Harlequin was a scamp and a trickster. Meeting Scaramouch, a musician, they danced and played their way through Italy until they arrived in Venice, prepared to make their fortune.

There, at Burattino's Inn, Harlequin heard of Columbine, whose beauty was matched only by her skill at dancing. But Columbine's father, a doctor of rather dubious ability, was possessive of his only child and kept her locked in the house. Violetta, a happy accomplice, and Pierrot an unhappy one, round out the cast of characters.

In traditional *Commedia dell'Arte* style the plot and counterplot build up to a most satisfying ending in this retelling of the classic story. Margot Zemach's rich illustrations, in bold black and rich plum, capture the essence of the lusty characters and settings reminiscent of Italy of the sixteenth century.

HARLEQUIN

ROSE LAURA MINCIELI

HARLEQUIN

PICTURES BY

MARGOT ZEMACH

New York : Alfred A. Knopf : 1968

This is a Borzoi book
published by Alfred A. Knopf, Inc.

 Distributed by Random House, Inc., New York, N. Y. Published simultaneously in Canada, by Random House of Canada Limited, Toronto. Manufactured in the United States of America.

Library of Congress Catalog Card Number: 67-15807

To my mother,
with ceaseless gratitude

FOREWORD

Harlequin, one of the most magical Italian theatrical figures ever created, has survived for over four hundred years. He has been inherited by the world of drama as a tradition, a personality, a character. This tradition is associated with the *maschera* or mask, each character in the old plays having a mask to wear.

There are many interpretations of the beginning of the Commedia dell' Arte, and here it is sufficient to say that these were traveling troupes of actors who set up their small platform stage in the market places of Italy. Sometimes these people were also traveling merchants, or members of a local guild. Gradually the costumes, the masks, even the gestures and speeches became a tradition.

The different types of masks, through long usage, became stereotyped. For example, in scenes depicting the relationship between a master and servant, the actor portraying the master's grumbling severity and suspicion wore a mask whose lines were frozen in a stern expression; the servant's dirt-streaked appearance was symbolized by a coal-smudged leather face piece. And so it was, with the purse-proud mistress and the saucy maid, the sighing daughter and her longing lover, the braggart soldier, all of whom wore the appropriate mask and costume of their role.

Here, in this version, Harlequin wears the full mask and beard of earlier times of the Italian performances. In the French version he is often portrayed with only a black eye mask.

Harlequin, Pantaloon, Pierrot, Captain Spavento, Columbine, Violetta—these names have traveled across language barriers, and are recognized as types.

The story of the maschera is so rich in tradition that the difficulty in writing this foreword has been what to omit. However, my aim will have been accomplished, if this thumbnail sketch will create a desire in the reader to know something more of the great heritage of the Commedia dell'Arte.

Rose Laura Mincieli

CONTENTS

HARLEQUIN

I

HARLEQUIN

Harlequin loved to dance. He flitted and glided along the streets like a leaf before an autumn wind. It was said that he danced before he could walk. And when he did, how lightly he walked.

Besides, he was a rascal. Whenever there was mischief in the making in the city of Bergamo, there was Harlequin in the middle of it. Soon he became the leader among boys who were, many of them, twice his size.

He climbed up church towers nimbly as a monkey and set the church bells ringing at the oddest times. No one could hope to catch him. He simply laughed at those who tried. And then, he scrambled down the tower like quicksilver and off and away he danced. In his multicolored suit of diamond-shaped patches, Harlequin pirouetted about the Italian streets like a fluttering butterfly making mischief wherever he went.

His mother laughed at his doings. His fat father, a fruit vendor, scolded him, but then secretly smiled as he thought of his own youthful days as a mischief-maker. "*Ahimè!* I was just such a *pidicino*—such a rascal—at his age," he would say.

That is, until he found out one day that Harlequin had been in the habit of sitting in the window above the shop eating cherries and tossing the pits out onto the customers. This form of amusement had so annoyed the customers that they began to buy their fruit elsewhere.

Now, his father became very angry. He went to the carpenter's shop and bought a stick of wood—long, thin, and flexible. And Harlequin, dancing into the shop one day, whistling and gay as usual, unexpectedly received his first thrashing.

"*Basta! Basta!* Enough! Enough!" he cried most loudly, for his father's arm was strong. His handsome clothes fitted him tightly and did not protect him from the sting of the whip.

Still, Harlequin lived for mischief-making, and the fun which he got out of making mischief was well worth an occasional whipping.

As Harlequin reached young manhood, it was thought that he would become less mischievous. Instead, he discovered

new kinds of tricks. One day there was a procession in Bergamo, a very magnificent affair. All the princes and merchants rode proudly on their horses, and the townspeople, bearing colorful banners, marched on foot. Among them was Harlequin's father, dressed in his best church-going suit with his gold watch chain strung proudly across his vest.

The procession was approaching the cathedral, and everything seemed to be going as it should. Suddenly there was a flash and a bang, then another, then a whole series of pops, and cracks, and bangs. The horses reared, threw their riders, and dashed into the crowd. Women screamed, men shouted, and all was confusion.

As Harlequin flung his last firecracker into an old woman's market basket, he paused a moment to laugh as she scuttled away as though the devil himself were after her. Then he slipped quickly up a deserted side street. He chuckled with glee for a minute over the excitement he had caused. Ahimè, it had been a pretty piece of mischief.

But those rearing horses and the sounds of confusion still coming from the square suddenly made him think that someone could have been hurt. Surely it would not take them long to guess who had thrown the firecrackers. Who but himself, the town's greatest mischief-maker? And if anyone were seriously hurt, he would certainly be held to account for it.

For the first time in his life, Harlequin was frightened. "I doubt whether the air of Bergamo will be good for my health for some time to come," he said to himself as he hurried back to the shop, which he knew would be empty, for his mother was in the great square, watching the procession. He filled a bag with fruit and took, as a weapon for protection, that long flexible stick with which he had had such painful experiences. He could not help shivering as he swished it through the air making it whistle.

Harlequin hid in an empty stable on the outskirts of the city until nightfall and, as soon as it was dark enough, he took to the road.

2

HARLEQUIN MEETS SCARAMOUCH

Harlequin walked on through the darkness. He whistled and skipped, and every now and then turned a somersault. Presently the moon rose, and it seemed to Harlequin that she was smiling at him. He took this for a good omen, and bowed to her respectfully, and then blew her an airy kiss.

He was not really very much worried by the idea of pursuit. In the first place, it was likely that the Bergamese, including his father, would be only too glad to get rid of him. In the second place, he knew that he could outdistance any pursuer, on foot or mounted. He threw up his heels at the very idea and turned another somersault.

About dawn he met two ruffians who attempted to rob him. But they were fat, slow-footed country fellows, and they could not even touch the agile Harlequin, who flew around and around them like a ring of flame. He had only his light stick against their clubs, but he made it whirl and flash so that they thought it was a sword of finest steel. He flicked one man on the cheek, who ran away screaming that he was dead. The other he caught across the ankles, and the fellow fell on his hands and knees and crawled off as fast as he could. So sure was he that both his feet were gone that he did not try to stand up until he had crawled for more than a mile.

Harlequin went on his way, munching one of his father's pears and whistling a merry tune whenever his mouth was empty.

At the first town he came to, he bought a leather mask and put it on. "Just in case my father should catch up with me," he thought.

Then, having bought sausages and wine with the few pennies in his pocket, he set out once more on his journey. He had not gone very far before he heard, coming from around the bend in the road ahead of him, the sound of such lively music that his feet were fairly caught up in the tune. When he came in sight of the lute player Harlequin was already dancing and pirouetting like a goat.

The player, seated by the roadside, kept on playing and

Harlequin kept on dancing till finally he reached the musician and made a low bow. Then the player laid down his lute hung with gay ribbons, and stared at Harlequin. He was a round-faced, rough-looking fellow, dressed all in black except for a white frill around his neck, and he wore a black cap rakishly on one side.

"*Buon giorno*. Who are you?" he asked.

Harlequin was too out of breath to think of anything but the truth. "Harlequin. And now, name for name, my friend."

"That is but fair," said the musician, rising to his feet, and making a ceremonious bow. "I am Scaramouch, at your service. You may have heard of me."

"I am afraid not," said Harlequin.

"*Scusi,*" replied Scaramouch, looking much surprised. "But where do you come from?"

"From Bergamo."

"Ah! that explains it. A poor city, where music has never been appreciated. You may have noticed," went on Scaramouch, boastfully throwing out his chest, "that I am something of a performer on the lute."

"Ah, yes," replied Harlequin. "Such playing I have never heard before."

Scaramouch smiled. "Thank you," he said. "I see that although a Bergamese, you are a person of unusual understanding. But I can honestly return your compliment. In all my wanderings, and I have visited the most famous cities of Italy, I have yet to meet one who dances so gracefully."

"*E vero?* Really?" Harlequin was delighted.

"*Si, vero*. No one," said Scaramouch. "*Benveduto,*" he continued. "We are a pair well met. Together, we will conquer the world."

"*Buono, buono,* that sounds good to me," said Harlequin, who was on the verge of turning another somersault.

"Then listen to me carefully. But, just a minute, you have not told me where you are going."

"Nowhere in particular," Harlequin replied. "I go where my feet take me."

"Then you could not travel in better company than mine," laughed Scaramouch. "For I have never yet found adventure far from me."

"But your plan?"

"It is simple enough. I am a musician, not only by nature, but by profession. With my lute, I earn my living. And, if you will permit me, or even if you do not, I think I am the greatest musician in all of Italy."

"Then you should be the wealthiest musician in all of Italy," said Harlequin.

"Ahime, I should be but I'm not. There are so few people who can appreciate music for its own sake. 'You play beautifully, Scaramouch,' they say, 'but what a pity you do not sing or dance as well. It would be so entertaining if you did.' But, unfortunately, I sing like a frog and dance like an elephant. Perhaps you can sing, Harlequin?"

"Not very well," answered Harlequin.

"What one cannot do very well is not worth doing at all," replied Scaramouch thoughtfully. "But with me to play and you to dance, we shall earn not twice, but ten times as much as I could earn alone. Are you ready to start?"

"To make my fortune? With all my heart. But where are we going to begin?"

"In Venice," said Scaramouch. "Venice is the place where fortunes are made. Why, the merchants there are richer than princes anywhere else."

"Good," replied Harlequin, turning a neat somersault.

"I see that you wear a mask. It will not come amiss to our work," Scaramouch added. "A touch of mystery always appeals to the spectators."

"Then let it be Venice," said Harlequin, executing a joyous pirouette.

3

AT BURATTINO'S INN

After many days of travel over the mountains east of Bergamo, through Verona and Padua, they finally arrived in Venice. And Harlequin not only liked Venice, as Scaramouch had predicted, but found it a most astonishing city.

Having never before been outside Bergamo, he had, of course, never seen so much water. Here was a city built on islets separated by many twisting canals, where stone houses had their feet in the water and people went about their business mostly in gondolas. There were also a few streets and a public square almost surrounded by water.

Scaramouch took Harlequin to an inn kept by a certain Burattino, where he had stayed many times before. In the doorway they were greeted by the innkeeper's daughter, Violetta. She was rosy-cheeked and plump and laced in a tight bodice above her full skirt.

"Buon giorno, Scaramouch," she said. "And who is your masked companion?"

"This is my young friend, Harlequin," replied Scaramouch. "A famous dancer."

"Benveduto," said Violetta. "Welcome." Then, turning to Scaramouch she commanded, "Play us a tune, Scaramouch. I want to see Harlequin dance."

So Scaramouch played, and Harlequin danced, and soon the girl joined in. They danced and danced, Harlequin pirouetting around and around until they were both out of breath.

Then when they stopped, Harlequin made a ceremonious bow before Violetta. "You dance beautifully, Violetta," he told her.

"*Ma che,* hardly the equal of Columbine. Ah! *There* is a dancer who dazzles the eye. She is worthy to dance even with you."

But before Violetta could say more, her father, who had been awakened from his afternoon nap by Scaramouch's music, came bustling out of the inner room.

"Scaramouch!" he shouted, greeting him. "I would know your playing anywhere. But I cannot guess who this young

man may be. He seems to be on such excellent terms with my daughter."

Scaramouch introduced Harlequin to Burattino. With the introduction out of the way, Scaramouch asked the innkeeper for two of his best beds.

"For as long as you like, my dear Scaramouch," said the innkeeper, and he hustled away to make the room ready.

At present there was only one person beside themselves staying at the inn, but he was a very magnificent individual indeed. A gaunt man dressed in military uniform, with a great sword at his side and an enormous mustache which he twirled nervously with his fingers. He did not look at all pleased to see the newcomers, and glared at them fiercely from under eyebrows which were fit companions to his mustache.

Scaramouch bowed to him in a mocking manner. The soldier nodded curtly.

"Who is that?" whispered Harlequin.

"That," replied Scaramouch, "is the most illustrious Captain Spavento of the Ducal Venetian Army. Before long, you will find out for yourself more about him, I am sure."

"Violetta," he continued, addressing himself to her, "bring some bread and cheese and a bottle of wine for my companion and myself. We are hungry and thirsty from tramping the roads."

Violetta left them and shortly returned with a round loaf of bread, a large piece of *pecorino* cheese, and a bottle of red wine.

It did not take long for the weary travelers to finish the feast. "Ah," said Scaramouch, smacking his lips, "that was good. And now for a little sleep."

"You are a lazy fellow," said Harlequin. "Certainly the food and wine were excellent, but I'm in a hurry to see the rest of Venice, which we are to conquer together."

Scaramouch's only answer was a snore.

Violetta laughed when she saw Scaramouch. "He makes music even when he is asleep," she said. "Are you asleep, too, Harlequin? It is so hard to tell with that mask of yours."

"No, Violetta, I am not asleep. Shall I dance for you again?" He leaped up from his chair and poised himself on his toes ready to perform even without Scaramouch's music.

Another dance was too much for Captain Spavento. The battlefield was his specialty—not the dance floor. Annoyed beyond patience with Harlequin's performance and jealous beyond words for not having his grace, Spavento rose from his chair. With a tremendous oath, rattling his sword and twisting his mustache faster than ever, he came striding across the room.

"Stop! No more dancing," he boomed.

This unexpected outburst of temper so startled Harlequin that he came down on his heels with a thump.

"And by what authority do you interfere with my dancing, old man?" exploded Harlequin, a gleam of mischief in his eyes.

This suggestion of being an old man made Spavento furious. Although he was but a battered soldier, he prided himself on his youthful appearance.

"Do you know to whom you are speaking, sir?" he shouted.

"Well," replied Harlequin, "my sleepy friend here did mention your name, but I have forgotten it."

"My name is Captain Spavento, of the army of his Most Glorious Majesty of Venice," he said proudly. "I should have thought that my fame, which has spread to the four corners of Europe, would have reached even your miserable ears. For I have slain thousands on the field of battle and hundreds on the dueling ground. Now, sir, you know by what authority I command you to stop your dancing."

"You are being silly, Spavento," said Violetta impatiently.

"And if I refuse to stop dancing," asked Harlequin, "what then?"

"Why, then," cried Spavento, "I shall be compelled to give you the soundest thrashing that you ever had in your life."

"Perhaps I had better stop dancing, after all," Harlequin said to Violetta.

"What!" she cried unbelievingly. "Do you mean to say that you are afraid of that windbag?"

"He seems to be a very ferocious warrior," Harlequin replied in mock seriousness.

Violetta looked perplexedly at Harlequin.

"Ah, ha!" said Spavento, twirling his mustache in triumph. "I thought I would soon make you see things my way."

"You mentioned a thrashing," said Harlequin. He raised his stick, bent it almost double, and let one end go again with a swish. "A pretty toy, is it not?" he said and advanced, smiling, towards the captain.

Spavento stepped back. The color suddenly left his cheeks, and even his mustache seemed to droop.

"My dear sir!" he cried. "That is a most dangerous thing to play with. Be careful!"

"You were talking of a thrashing," Harlequin began again.

"But you misunderstood me," the soldier interrupted, through chattering teeth. "I assure you, you quite misunderstood me. I was only joking."

"I am something of a joker myself," said Harlequin. His eyes twinkling, he swung the stick over Spavento's head, missing it by a bare inch.

Violetta clapped her hands.

Spavento backed up step by step. Harlequin followed him. Once the stick just tweaked the captain's ear. He set up such a cry that it awakened Scaramouch, who all this time had been peacefully asleep.

"What is the matter?" he asked, stretching himself and yawning. "Oh, I see—the captain. I told you you would soon find him out, Harlequin."

Seeing Harlequin's attention for a moment diverted, Spavento made a dash for the door and up the stairs to his room. He did not appear again that evening. But the next day, he was back in his accustomed place, entertaining Burattino's new customers with a story of the terrible thrashing which he had given Harlequin.

However, whenever Scaramouch or Violetta or Harlequin himself happened to be in the room, the captain was seized with a sudden fit of coughing.

4

HOW HARLEQUIN FIRST SAW COLUMBINE

Scaramouch seemed to be in no hurry to start making that fortune of which he had talked so eloquently to Harlequin. But the two artists were not altogether idle. Every evening they played and danced for the amusement of the company in the inn. With the few *liras* they earned by their performance, they were able to pay for their keep at the inn.

Soon their skill was the talk of Venice. Harlequin became

as famous as Scaramouch; people came to see him, and Burattino rubbed his fat hands with delight as his business flourished. Everyone was pleased except Spavento, to whose tales of valorous deeds no one would listen when the musician and the dancer performed.

One day, while Harlequin sat talking with Scaramouch, he heard Violetta calling him.

"Harlequin!" she cried. "Come here to the window. Quickly!"

"What is it?" he asked.

"Pantaloon and Columbine are passing."

Harlequin hurried to the window.

"There they go," said Violetta. "Isn't she lovely?"

She was very lovely, Harlequin thought. He had never seen anyone like her. Violetta was pretty, but Columbine was beautiful. There was no other word for her. She was rather small and every feature was most exquisitely made. Her complexion was of the daintiest pink and white like a Dresden doll; her hair, a great golden coil around her beautiful little head, gleamed in the sunshine. Except for the rosebuds in her tiny straw hat, Columbine was dressed all in white, and her skirt was of some light gossamer fabric which seemed to float its wearer through the air.

Harlequin remembered that Violetta had said Columbine would be worthy to dance even with him.

"With me as her partner, I would lead her in many whirls," he said. "She seems light-footed enough. See, she hardly touches the ground at all."

Watching her till she was out of sight, he had no eyes for

her companion. Yet Pantaloon, in his own way, was well worth looking at, for he was as ugly as his daughter was beautiful, as ungainly as she was graceful. Wrapped in his faded doctor's cloak, with his huge spectacles on his great beak of a nose, he stomped along at her side, leaning heavily on his silver-headed cane.

"Well," asked Violetta, "what do you think of her?"

"She is beautiful. Why, she is more like a fairy than a girl," replied Harlequin.

"All the same, I would not be her for a thousand gold pieces," Violetta said. "She is shut up all day in a little house with no one to talk to but her old father and that foolish Pierrot."

"Who is her father?" asked Harlequin. "And who is Pierrot?"

"Columbine's father is Pantaloon, the doctor, and Pierrot is his assistant. Though of what assistance he can be I am unable to imagine, for his wits are always in the clouds. Pantaloon is an old villain. He has always guarded Columbine as closely as though she were a princess. Why, he lets no one come near her, except myself," said Violetta.

"Poor Columbine," whispered Harlequin, shaking his head.

"Yes, poor Columbine. Pantaloon is determined that she shall marry no one but Lelio, a rich man of his own choosing. Of course, it would be a fine thing for him to have a rich nobleman for a son-in-law. He would be able to shut up his books and retire, which would be the best thing—for all that he knows about medicine."

"Does he ever let Columbine out of the house?" asked Harlequin.

"Never, except to walk in his own company. I suppose he is afraid that she would otherwise grow fat, and lose her beauty. They pass this way occasionally, for their house is only at the end of the street—the gray stone house near the *piazza*."

"Poor Columbine," again said Harlequin.

"Yes, poor Columbine," repeated Violetta. And away she went to her work in the kitchen, humming a merry little tune.

5

HARLEQUIN VISITS THE DOCTOR

Next morning, Harlequin slipped out of the inn and walked as far as Pantaloon's house.

He saw the closed door and the heavily slatted shutters, through which, even if Columbine were standing behind them, there was not the least chance of catching a glimpse of her. And he did so want to see her.

"How on earth does one get into a house without an excuse?" Harlequin asked himself. Then he remembered that Pantaloon was a doctor.

"Why," he cried, "what a simpleton I am!"

Harlequin twisted his face into an expression of pain and knocked at the door.

Three times he had to knock, and even then it was only after a great rattling of chains and creaking of bolts that the door was opened slightly. A long white face peered through the narrow opening, a face made all the whiter by the black skullcap which crowned it, a pair of big sad eyes, and a little scarlet mouth shaped like an O. This, as Harlequin immediately guessed, was Pierrot.

"What do you want?" asked a quavering voice, no louder than a whisper.

"I am very ill," said Harlequin. "I want to see Doctor Pantaloon."

"Oh, do you?" questioned Pierrot. "Are you really very ill?"

"Dreadfully," said Harlequin. "I feel as though I am about to die."

"Well," said Pierrot doubtfully, "I will ask him if he will see you. He doesn't see everyone, you know."

He shut the door in Harlequin's face.

"What a heartless fellow!" thought Harlequin. "For all he cares I could die in the street."

Presently Pierrot opened the door again.

"Come in," he said. "This way."

He led Harlequin into an untidy room, surrounded by shelves full of curious objects and bottles containing liquids of various colors. From the ceiling hung a stuffed crocodile. Pierrot then withdrew to his workbench and mortar and pestle to mix the doctor's medicines. There he sat in his loose, long white suit and from time to time glanced quizzically at Harlequin.

Harlequin looked about the room with much curiosity, wondering what he had let himself in for.

After a few minutes, Pantaloon came stomping in. He glared fiercely at Harlequin through his large spectacles.

"Well," he said gruffly, "what do you want?"

"I am very ill," Harlequin repeated.

"Why do you come to me?" asked Pantaloon suspiciously. "You are not one of my regular patients."

"But one cannot very well be a regular patient," replied Harlequin, "until one has paid you a first visit. Can one?"

"No," said Pantaloon thoughtfully, "that is true enough."

"I like to have the best of everything," continued Harlequin. "So, naturally, being ill, I came to you."

"Quite so, quite so," said Pantaloon, more amiably than he had yet spoken. "But who told you to come to me?"

"Why," cried Harlequin, "all Venice. For all Venice talks of the skill and learning of Doctor Pantaloon."

The doctor smiled, or at any rate turned up the corners of his mouth. "Well, young man," he said, "I will do what I can for you. Let me look at your tongue."

Harlequin put out his tongue and Pantaloon peered at it.

"Horrible!" he exclaimed. "I am afraid you are very ill. Let me feel your pulse."

He took Harlequin's wrist in one hand, and an enormous watch from his pocket in the other.

"Ahimè!" he exclaimed, "what a rate it is going."

Harlequin noticed, however, that whatever his pulse was doing, the watch was not going at all.

"Have you any pain?" asked the doctor.

"Yes," said Harlequin, "a horrible pain." And he rubbed his stomach.

"It is a good thing you came to me," said Pantaloon. "There is no one else in Venice who could save your life."

He took a bottle down from one of the shelves, and poured some pink liquid into a glass. To this he added some green and then a little purple. It made a pretty colored mixture.

"Drink this," he commanded Harlequin.

"May I take it home with me?" asked Harlequin hopefully, for he had only wanted a chance to see Columbine, not to drink a horrible medicine.

"Certainly not," replied Pantaloon. "All depends on your drinking it—immediately."

So Harlequin closed his eyes and swallowed the medicine down quickly; there was nothing else he could do. He twisted his face up even more when he had finished the drink.

"Ahimè!" he exclaimed.

"That will make you feel much better," said Pantaloon.

"It has made me feel much worse," the patient retorted, sinking into a chair and clasping his head in his hands. "Oh, my poor head!" he cried.

"What is the matter with it?" asked Pantaloon.

"It aches terribly," said Harlequin.

"That is just as it should be," said Pantaloon, nodding his head knowingly. "The medicine has driven the pain upwards.

In a minute or two it will come out at the top and you will be all right."

"Your horrible medicine has made me feel worse," cried Harlequin, for truthfully it really had.

"Ma che!" the doctor shouted, feeling insulted. "It is the most excellent medicine in the world—far too good to be poured down your worthless throat. Now, be off with you."

"Gladly!" exclaimed Harlequin, and made for the door.

"Not so fast," cried Pantaloon. "Before you go, I want my fee. One lira."

"One lira!" exclaimed Harlequin. "One lira for that vile potion? You ought to pay me for drinking it."

"*Contadino!* You peasant! If you don't pay me," shouted Pantaloon, in a threatening voice, "I will call the *carabiniere* and have you arrested for the rogue you are."

Harlequin realized that there was nothing to be gained by making the doctor any angrier, so he reluctantly gave him one lira and took his departure.

Pierrot, silent and melancholy as ever, let him out of the house.

Harlequin had to admit to himself that his visit had not been successful. He had failed to see Columbine, had almost made an enemy of her father and, besides, had been forced to pay a lira for the most horrible drink he had ever tasted.

6

VIOLETTA SETS HER WITS TO WORK

"Where have you been all this time?" asked Violetta, as Harlequin entered the inn.

"Nowhere in particular," said Harlequin carelessly.

"I wouldn't mind betting twenty liras that he has been trying to see Columbine," Violetta said to Scaramouch.

"And I wouldn't mind betting fifty that he has not succeeded," replied Scaramouch.

"Did you, Harlequin?" Violetta asked.

"No, I didn't," Harlequin admitted. "But I made the acquaintance of her papa."

"I am sure he was not glad to make yours," said Scaramouch. "He is not noted for his hospitality."

"He certainly insisted on giving me medicine," said Harlequin, making a sour face.

"What happened, Harlequin?" asked Violetta, curious to know the details.

So Harlequin told them, and before he had finished both Scaramouch and Violetta were nearly dying of laughter.

"I don't think it was as funny as all that," said Harlequin sulkily.

"Ahimè Harlequin," said Violetta. "What a shame. But I would have thought you were too clever to attempt making Columbine's acquaintance in such a simple way."

"Well," said Harlequin, "since Columbine hardly ever goes outside the house, I thought my best chance of meeting her was to get inside."

"We will all have to put our heads together and think of a way for you to meet Columbine," said Violetta firmly.

"Is it absolutely necessary that he do so?" Scaramouch asked.

"Of course it is," replied Violetta. "How else can he dance with her?"

"Violetta, if I could only dance with her!" exclaimed Harlequin.

"But Columbine might not like to dance with *you,*" teased Scaramouch.

"Nonsense!" retorted Violetta.

"Violetta, you are a friend," cried Harlequin.

"Well," said Scaramouch, "I may as well help. So, why don't you try again when Pantaloon is out?"

"That won't work," said Violetta scornfully. "Pantaloon very rarely goes out—except when he is summoned to a patient. And when he does go, Pierrot keeps the door locked. Poor Harlequin. I pity you. You don't seem to be able to help yourself. But I have an idea that I can."

"Have you?" asked Harlequin eagerly. "Tell me."

"Well," said Violetta, "the important thing is that Columbine should see you dancing. She adores dancing more than anything else in the world, though it is not much that she gets of it, poor girl. There is no one to dance with her, and I am sure she little enjoys dancing alone. Pierrot, though he sings very nicely, can't dance a bit. So to see a dancer like you, Harlequin, would be a wonderful treat for her. And if you could only perform together, she would be yours forever."

"Ahimè! That would be wonderful," sighed Harlequin. "But how is it to be managed? How can we ever dance together?"

"We must think about *that* later," said Violetta. "It is no use being impatient; we must take one step at a time. If only we can manage to have her *see* you dancing—*that* would be an achievement."

"But can we?" Harlequin asked.

"I think so," Violetta answered. "You can dance in the street as well as in the house, I suppose?"

"Of course," replied Harlequin.

"And Columbine can look out of the window," said Violetta. "The point is to get her to look out of the window at the same time that you are dancing in the street."

"That ought to be easy," said Harlequin.

"It isn't the least bit easy," replied Violetta. "How are we to let her know that you are going to be there?"

"By sending her a letter, I suppose," said Harlequin.

"By sending her a letter," repeated Violetta, exasperated. "Why, Pantaloon would be the first to see it. All the same, a letter it must be—only it mustn't be *sent;* it must be delivered straight into Columbine's own hands—by someone we can trust."

"Whom can we trust?" asked Harlequin impatiently.

"Only ourselves," said Violetta. "You—I—and Scaramouch. At least I suppose we can trust you, Scaramouch?"

"You can," replied the musician.

"But which of us is to deliver the letter?" questioned Harlequin.

"Well, you have seen what luck you had when you tried to visit her," said Violetta. "And Scaramouch would fare no better. It is plain that it will have to be me."

"Ah, will you?" cried Harlequin.

"I will try, anyway," the girl replied. "But it is not going to be easy even for me. Besides the letter, there is another problem."

"Ahimè!" exclaimed Harlequin. "There seems to be no end to the difficulties. What is this one?"

"Pantaloon himself," said Violetta. "Of course, he must be out of the house if Columbine is to watch Harlequin dance.

Possibly on a sick call. But, first things first. I will deliver a letter to Columbine. Somehow I shall find a way to give it to her."

"Oh, Violetta, you are wonderful," said Harlequin, who was so happy over the possibility of dancing with Columbine that he immediately started pirouetting around Violetta.

7

VIOLETTA AT PANTALOON'S HOUSE

So, Violetta set out for Pantaloon's house. She did not tell Harlequin and Scaramouch exactly what she meant to do.

"Buon giorno, Pierrot," she said, when the doctor's sad-faced assistant had opened the door for her. "Good day."

"Buon giorno, Violetta," sorrowfully replied Pierrot. "What brings you here? I hope you are not ill."

"Dear me, no," replied Violetta. "I only want to see

Columbine for a moment, here at the doorway."

"She is busy," said Pierrot doubtfully.

"Tell her I have a beautiful scarf to give her," Violetta said. "I'll only stay a minute."

"Couldn't I take it to her?" Pierrot asked.

"Oh, no, Pierrot, you have such a weak head," said Violetta. "Why, you would go dreaming along and forget to give it to her."

"You have a very poor opinion of me, haven't you, Violetta?" said Pierrot in a mournful voice.

"Now don't stand there arguing," cried Violetta. "Run along and bring Columbine."

So, Pierrot went for Columbine and returned with her. As soon as Pierrot turned his back, Violetta gave Columbine a warm smile and beckoned her to come close.

"Here, take this," she whispered. And pressed a folded piece of paper into Columbine's hand which she had kept concealed in the scarf. "Hide it quickly and keep the scarf!"

Columbine thrust the note into the pocket of her dress and looked perplexed.

Hastily saying good-by, Violetta took her leave. Columbine hurried back to her room. She wanted to be alone to read that mysterious note.

It was a very short note. This was all it said:

Next time your father goes out
and you are alone in the room,
look out of the window
at the side of the house.

Nothing more—not even a signature. Columbine, who had never received such a mysterious message before, found it exciting. What could it mean? She would certainly do as it told her, though unfortunately, she reflected, she might have to wait a long time. Sometimes her father did not leave the house for days. Columbine could not help hoping that her father would be summoned on a sick call soon.

The door opened and Pierrot entered. Columbine quickly hid the note in her pocket.

"My eyes can see a long way, Columbine," was all he said.

"What did you see?" she asked.

Pierrot smiled sadly and said, "Maybe I should tell your father."

"Oh, Pierrot!" cried the girl, in panic. "You wouldn't do that!"

"It may be my duty," said Pierrot solemnly. "I always like to do my duty."

"But what *did* you see?" Columbine repeated.

Pierrot only raised his eyebrows.

"I don't believe you saw anything at all," said Columbine. "You are teasing me."

"It is not always what one sees, my dear," Pierrot began more sadly.

"I am not your dear," interrupted Columbine, stamping her foot in annoyance.

"Yes, you are," said Pierrot. "You may not think you are—but you are. But to go on with what I was saying when you interrupted me—it is not always what one sees that is

important; it is what one feels. And I feel that there is mischief going on."

"I hope there *is,*" said Columbine rebelliously.

"Oh, Columbine!" said Pierrot, shocked.

"Well," said Columbine, "it is about time something happened. I am sick and tired of being cooped-up here with nothing to do, never going anywhere, and seeing no one but you and Papa."

"And Lelio," Pierrot added.

"Oh, don't talk to me about Lelio," said Columbine, frowning.

"I don't *want* to talk of him," said Pierrot. "He is no friend of mine. He treats me badly."

"It's a shame," cried Columbine.

"I don't really mind that," said Pierrot mournfully. "I am used to it. It doesn't matter how he treats me. But he is going to take you away. I could never forgive him for that."

"He is going to do nothing of the kind," said Columbine decidedly. "I will never marry Lelio, Pierrot."

"All the same, I am sure there is mischief afoot," said Pierrot. "I feel it in my bones."

"I don't know where else you would feel it," Columbine scoffed. "You are nothing else but bones."

"Cruel Columbine," sighed Pierrot.

Columbine danced around the room.

"Will you do something for me?"

"Anything in the world," said Pierrot.

"Then," said Columbine, "promise me that whatever you have guessed, and whatever you notice during the next few days, you will say nothing to Papa."

"Oh, Columbine!" cried Pierrot, "you are not going to do anything dreadful?"

"I don't know what I am going to do," Columbine laughed. "I don't know what is going to happen. But promise."

"I promise," said Pierrot.

8

HARLEQUIN DANCES FOR COLUMBINE

Violetta returned to the inn, well pleased with the success of her scheme. She found the others waiting for her, and told them what she had accomplished.

"Bravo!" cried Scaramouch. "You are a clever girl, Violetta, to think of hiding the letter in a scarf."

As for Harlequin, he was so delighted that he danced about the room and made Violetta dance with him until she was breathless, and ready to sit down.

"You should save your breath for dancing for Columbine," she panted, when at last he stopped.

"I am ready to begin now," cried Harlequin, who could dance all day without tiring. "What about a plan for getting old Pantaloon out of the way, Scaramouch?"

"It would be too late to carry it out this evening," replied the musician.

"Ma che!" exclaimed Harlequin, "It is never too late."

"You mustn't be so impatient, Harlequin," said Violetta. "It is nearly dark—and what on earth would be the use of your dancing before Columbine's window if she could not see you?"

Harlequin had to agree, so he made up his mind to wait till the morning with as much patience as he could command. But he was far too excited to sleep. He spent half the night inventing new and fantastic dance steps, to the annoyance of Scaramouch, who shared the bedroom with him.

"If you don't stop jigging about and get into bed, I won't lift a finger to help you," yawned the sleepy musician.

That quieted Harlequin, but though he lay down, he did not go to sleep, and he dragged his friend out of bed at a very early hour.

After breakfast, over which Scaramouch absolutely refused to hurry, in spite of Harlequin's growing impatience, the musician told the dancer to go and hide near Pantaloon's house.

"Be sure," he added, "that you choose a spot where you cannot be seen, but from which you can see who goes in and

out of the house, and which way they go."

Harlequin picked up his stick and skipped away.

Presently, Spavento came down from his room, swaggered in, and sat at a table. He then sent Violetta into the kitchen to bring him his breakfast.

Scaramouch strolled across to his table.

"Buon giorno, my dear Captain," he said seriously. "I *hope* you are feeling well this fine morning."

"Perfectly well, I thank you, sir," replied Spavento, greatly surprised at the other's unusual concern.

"I am glad to hear you say so," said Scaramouch, in a doubtful tone. "Very glad indeed. In fact, I am much relieved."

"Why?" cried Spavento. "Don't I look well?"

"Since you ask me," said Scaramouch, "I must confess that you don't. In my opinion, you look far from well."

These words alarmed the captain, which was exactly what the musician had hoped they would do. For Scaramouch had guessed that Spavento was as big a coward about his health as he was in other ways.

"Ahimè," said the unhappy captain, "now that you mention it, I really don't think that I am feeling well."

"I should say that you are not," said Scaramouch.

"Yes," said Spavento. "I am afraid I am not."

At that moment Violetta entered with his breakfast.

"Take it away," groaned Spavento. "I cannot look at it."

"Why, Captain," Violetta asked, "what is the matter?"

"I am much too ill to eat anything," said Spavento.

"Ill?" said the girl in surprise, for she did not know what Scaramouch was planning. "It is nothing catching, I hope?"

"I don't know what it is," moaned the soldier. "I wish I did."

"I think you ought to send for the doctor, my friend," said Scaramouch.

"Yes, I think I ought to," agreed Spavento. "But who?"

"Why, for Pantaloon, of course," said Scaramouch, winking at Violetta who, immediately understanding what was afoot, winked gleefully back. "He is the best doctor in Venice. Besides, he lives so near. Let me get him for you."

"Would you?" asked Spavento, slumping in his chair as though about to faint.

"Say no more," replied Scaramouch heartily. "Now just go back to bed, and I will soon have Doctor Pantaloon here to see you."

Harlequin, in the meantime, had been in hiding, watching Pantaloon's house from a distance. He saw Scaramouch arrive at the doctor's door which, after the usual delay, was opened by Pierrot. Scaramouch went inside, but it was not long before he came out again and, to the dancer's joy, he was accompanied by Pantaloon.

The doctor, in fact, had not hesitated to visit Spavento. Knowing him only by sight, he judged him from his clothes to be a very fine gentleman, and wealthy. He hurried towards the inn as fast as his gouty legs would carry him. And luckily he did not look around, or he would have seen Harlequin blowing him a farewell kiss. Harlequin ran towards the window at which Violetta had previously told him he might see Columbine.

He looked up at the window, and he was not disappointed. For no sooner had Columbine heard the door close behind her father and his visitor than she had made haste to follow the instructions contained in Violetta's mysterious and exciting letter. So Harlequin had a glimpse of a golden head peeping timidly from behind the partly opened shutters.

Then he began to dance—as never before in his life. The hope of pleasing Columbine inspired him to something better than his best. He found himself doing twists, whirls, and leaps into the air, dazzling steps which he had never done before. Tunes came into his head more melodious than any that had ever flowed from Scaramouch's lute, and his feet followed them of their own accord.

From time to time he watched Columbine's window. At first he could see nothing but a flash of golden hair. Little by little, however, the shutters parted, and presently the casement window was thrown open, and Columbine, her timidity lost in wonder and delight, leaned far out over the sill. She leaned so far out of the window that Harlequin grew nervous and stopped dancing. Then Harlequin made his most graceful bow.

"*Ecco, Signorina,*" he said, "how did you like it?"

"Oh, it was perfect," cried Columbine. "I have never seen dancing like that before. But who are you? What is your name?"

Harlequin told her.

"I know yours," he added.

"Do you?" said Columbine. But her thoughts were still on the wonderful dancing.

"I never imagined anyone could dance like that," she said.

"Ah, but you could yourself," said Harlequin.

"Oh, no!" Columbine protested.

"Violetta says you could," Harlequin replied. "She told me that you love dancing."

"I do," cried Columbine, "above all things. But I can't dance as you do."

"Try," said Harlequin. "Let us dance together."

"How can we?" Columbine asked. "I can't get out."

"But I could get in the window," said Harlequin, "if you would let down a rope."

"Oh, I dare not!" cried Columbine.

"Well, then," said Harlequin, "I will dance down here, and you shall dance up there. How would that be?"

"It sounds like great fun. Let us do that," said Columbine, much relieved.

So Harlequin began dancing again, and Columbine, after watching him for a while, joined in. She followed him perfectly, repeating even his most intricate movements with shimmering grace.

They were still dancing, he on the ground and she at the window, when Violetta appeared on the scene. She clapped her hands in admiration, and then she put one hand on Harlequin's shoulder.

"That was very pretty," she cried, "but you must stop now. Pantaloon will soon be here."

Harlequin, who was bubbling with cheerfulness, called up to Columbine, "I shall come again, and next time you must have the rope ready." As he bowed low, he added softly, "You dance exquisitely, Signorina." And his eyes flashed beneath his mask.

"Do I, Harlequin?" Columbine softly asked.

"Of course you do," said Harlequin.

Columbine blushed. Her cheeks turned rosy—as before they had been white.

"Hurry! Hurry!" interrupted Violetta, "you really must come away."

"Very well," said Harlequin reluctantly. "Good-by, Columbine. *Arrivederci.*"

"Good-by, Harlequin."

Violetta led Harlequin up a side street. As they made their way homewards, she gave him an account of the doctor's interview with Spavento, to which she had listened through the door. "It really was very funny," she said.

Pantaloon had kept asking Spavento what was the matter with him, and Spavento, of course, had been unable to say. But Scaramouch, who was with the captain, kept suggesting all sorts of aches and pains. No sooner had he mentioned them than Spavento was quite sure that he felt them. In the end, Pantaloon had decided that the captain was very ill indeed, and ordered him to stay in bed until his next visit.

"But I don't believe you are listening," said Violetta, annoyed.

"I am, Violetta, I am," protested Harlequin, who, as a matter of fact, had not been listening very closely, for his mind kept wandering back to Columbine's dancing. "You said something about Pantaloon's next visit, didn't you?"

"Yes," said Violetta. "He is going to call on Spavento again tomorrow morning."

"*Bravo! Bravo!*" Harlequin cried. He threw his stick high into the air and neatly caught it as it fell. "I shall be able to go to see Columbine again."

"Yes," said Violetta, "and I shouldn't be surprised if you were able to do so for several days."

"Do you really think so?" cried Harlequin. "Oh, Violetta, how wonderful! Let us dance the rest of the way home."

"No, thank you!" said Violetta emphatically. "*I* don't feel like dancing."

Harlequin looked at her in surprise. Imagine anyone not wanting to dance, he thought.

PIERROT SINGS TO COLUMBINE

As soon as Harlequin was out of sight, Pierrot entered Columbine's room. Startled, she turned. He gazed at her reproachfully out of his big, sad eyes.

"I was watching, too," he said. "From downstairs."

"Indeed," said Columbine calmly. "I hope you enjoyed yourself."

"Enjoyed myself," cried Pierrot. "As if I could, with that

fellow dancing outside. He made me feel so tired."

"What nonsense you talk, Pierrot," Columbine cried.

"I wish it were nonsense," said Pierrot.

Columbine stamped her foot.

"You are very impertinent," she cried, angrily.

"Do you know who the fellow is?" Pierrot asked her.

Columbine did not reply.

"There," said Pierrot, "you talk out of the window with someone about whom you know nothing."

"I do know something about him," said Columbine defiantly. "I know his name, anyway. It's Harlequin."

"And a queer name it is," Pierrot retorted. "Then look at his strange clothes. And why, I should like to know, does he wear a mask? I saw the fellow a few days ago, you know."

"I think his clothes are beautiful," said Columbine, "and his mask is very becoming. And he dances so gracefully."

"Oh, Columbine," said Pierrot mournfully.

"I wish you would try to look a little more cheerful," said Columbine. "Sing me something. Haven't you composed a new song lately?"

"Yes," Pierrot answered. "I composed one last week. I don't suppose you will like it."

"I can't tell until I have heard it, can I? "said Columbine. "Sing it to me."

So, in his melancholy voice, to a melancholy, wandering tune, Pierrot sang his song:

A swallow, one day
Flew across the blue

When he saw his mate;
Now they fly to the south
To nest as their fate.

Toward the end, Pierrot's voice trailed away into silence.

"What a strange fellow you are, Pierrot," said Columbine. "And what strange songs you sing."

At that moment Pantaloon's harsh voice was heard calling from downstairs. "Pierrot, Pierrot, where are you? There is medicine to prepare."

10

CAPTAIN SPAVENTO MAKES MISCHIEF

Upon repeated visits, Pantaloon found Spavento's illness very puzzling. Usually, all he had to do was to tell his patients in long words what they had told him in short ones, concoct a mixture from his bottles of medicines, and pocket his fee.

But Spavento could only repeat what Scaramouch suggested, and Scaramouch's suggestions were so astonishing, and varied so from day to day, that the poor doctor was quite bewildered. He felt that even if he mixed together the contents of all the bottles on his shelves, the concoction would not cure so complicated a case.

Nevertheless, he continued to visit the captain every morning.

And every morning Harlequin danced outside Columbine's window, while she danced behind it.

Pierrot, watching from a lower window, unnoticed by Harlequin, grew more and more disturbed. He was fearful that Pantaloon would return at any moment.

Harlequin never ceased trying to persuade Columbine to let down a rope to him. For several days she only shook her head, but at last she yielded. Pierrot, leaning out of the window one day and looking upwards, saw the dancer's legs disappear into the room above. He cast up his eyes and threw up his hands in despair.

Harlequin took Columbine's hand in his. Then they began to dance together, and never before had either of them so enjoyed dancing or danced so beautifully.

Violetta, coming as usual to warn Harlequin of Pantaloon's return, and not seeing him anywhere, wondered what had happened. She thought for a moment that he must have quarreled with Columbine and had gone away. When she caught sight through the wide-open window of the two dancing together, she was as horrified as Pierrot.

"Harlequin! Harlequin!" she called loudly. "How can you be so reckless? Come down at once. Pantaloon will be here any moment."

Reluctant as he was, Harlequin knew that delay could

mean trouble. With one last, long glance at Columbine, he slid down the rope. As soon as he was on the ground, Columbine quickly drew up the rope through the window.

As they walked back to the inn, Violetta scolded Harlequin for his daring. But she might have spared her breath. For, from that day forward, the rope was always let down, and Harlequin and Columbine passed many a happy hour dancing together.

One evening, as he lay in bed wondering how much longer he had to live, Spavento heard Harlequin and Scaramouch talking in low tones directly under his room. He could not make out what they were saying, but more than once he thought he heard his own name mentioned. This so aroused his curiosity that at last, in spite of the doctor's orders and his own fear of the consequences, he rose from his bed. Kneeling down on the floor, he put his ear to a crack between the boards.

What he heard filled him at once with rage. Scaramouch was entertaining his friend with a description of Pantaloon's visits and boasting of his own cleverness in keeping up the pretense of the captain's illness. When he learned the reason for the trick—which he soon did, for Harlequin could not long refrain from singing Columbine's praises—the captain rubbed his hands gleefully. Here was his chance to even the score. Harlequin should be well paid for having humiliated him at their first meeting.

Spavento returned to his bed. Now that he knew he had never really been ill at all, he felt very well. So he waited for Pantaloon, and when the doctor arrived, he invented an excuse for getting Scaramouch out of the room. And then he told

the doctor what he had overheard.

Pantaloon's anger knew no limit. He grew purple in the face; he raved and sputtered until Spavento became very frightened. When Pantaloon had recovered himself a little, his first thought was to rush off at once and catch Harlequin dancing with Columbine. But, suddenly, a new idea struck him, and he turned to Spavento.

"Since you are not ill after all," he said, "there will be no need for me to visit you anymore."

"No," replied Spavento, "of course not."

"Well, then," said Pantaloon, "I think you may as well pay me my fee now. Let me see—it will cost you . . ."

"*Un momento!* Just a minute," interrupted the captain. "Your fee is no affair of mine. It was not *I* who called you in, and you have done nothing for me. You had better present your bill to Scaramouch."

"I doubt that I could get a penny out of that scoundrel!" cried Pantaloon.

"Then what about Harlequin?" said Spavento.

"He is another scoundrel!" roared Pantaloon.

"Well then, you do not deserve a fee," replied Spavento, "for you are a doctor who does not even know whether his patient is ill or not."

"That is no worse than a patient who does not know it himself," Pantaloon replied.

"In that case," said Spavento, laughing foolishly, "perhaps we are even."

"We are not even until you have paid my fee," said Pantaloon.

"How can I pay your fee when I have no money?" Spavento asked.

"No money!" exclaimed the doctor in surprise. "Why, you are a wealthy nobleman, are you not?"

"I am a nobleman, it is true," replied Spavento, although it was not true at all. "And I should be wealthy. But I'm not."

"You, too, are a scoundrel!" shouted Pantaloon, his face turning purple once more.

This was too much for the haughty captain. "What!" he cried. "Do you dare to insult Spavento, you ignorant apothecary?" And, springing out of bed, he caught up his sword which had been placed on a nearby chair.

Even in his nightgown, the soldier, with his bristling mustache, his rolling eyes, and his long sword, was a terrifying figure, and the doctor, forgetting both his fee and his gout, made a dash for the door. Down the stairs he fled, and out into the street.

Violetta, busy in the kitchen and not expecting him to leave for another half hour at least, did not see him go.

II

COLUMBINE'S PUNISHMENT AND HARLEQUIN'S NEW PLAN

Harlequin and Columbine were happily dancing when Pierrot burst into the room with a look of alarm on his long pale face.

"Fly, Harlequin! You must fly at once!" he cried. "Pantaloon is letting himself into the house."

"Ahime!" cried Harlequin, and Columbine uttered a little shriek.

"Hush," whispered Pierrot. "He will hear you. For

heaven's sake, go, Harlequin. There is not a moment to lose."

Harlequin sprang to the window, where the rope by which he had entered still hung.

"You must come with me, Columbine, and be my wife," he said.

"Oh, no!" said poor Columbine. "I dare not."

"But I will look after you, my dear," pleaded Harlequin.

"I know you would, Harlequin," replied Columbine. "But I'm afraid."

They heard the front door slam, and Pantaloon clomping heavily up the stairs.

"You really must get out, Harlequin," said Pierrot.

"Yes," said Columbine. "Please go."

Harlequin hesitated another moment, and then, realizing that he would only make matters worse by staying, vaulted over the window sill and slid down the rope. Just as he reached the ground, Pantaloon opened Columbine's door.

In spite of his spectacles, the doctor's vision was not good and, seeing Pierrot standing by Columbine's side, he thought that he had caught the villain whom he was after.

"Ah, ha, I've got you, you scoundrel!" he roared, and rushed at his assistant with uplifted cane.

"Stop! Papa, that is only Pierrot," said Columbine.

"Why, so it is," said Pantaloon in surprise. "Get back to your work," he bellowed.

Pierrot, who was as timid as a mouse, crept out of the room and back to the apothecary jars.

When he had gone, Pantaloon began shouting at his daughter. "That scoundrel Harlequin has been here, I know

he has. You cannot fool me."

Columbine did not know what to say. So she said nothing.

"Perhaps he has not left," her father continued angrily. "Perhaps he is hiding here somewhere."

He began to look here and there and everywhere in the room, but, of course, he did not find Harlequin. Then he looked out into the street, but he did not see Harlequin there either, for the dancer was already halfway back to Burattino's inn. What Pantaloon did see, however, was the rope which Columbine had not had a chance to pull in and hide.

"Ah, ha!" he cried. "So this is the means by which that rascal visits you, is it? You disobedient girl! A rope! You deserve to be soundly whipped with the end of it."

The enraged father stormed and bellowed, shouted and threatened. When finally he had finished, Pantaloon stomped out of Columbine's room slamming the door behind him, leaving her weeping bitterly.

After a while, she heard a light tapping on the door.

"Who is it?" she asked.

"It is I, Pierrot," came the answer in a whisper. "Don't cry, Columbine. It will all come out right, I am sure. I will do all I can to help you."

"But what can you do, Pierrot?" said Columbine. "Oh, I am so miserable! I know I shall never see Harlequin again."

"You shall, you shall," said Pierrot. "I have already thought of a scheme. I dare not stay to tell it to you now. But trust Pierrot, Columbine."

"I will," Columbine answered. "Dear Pierrot, you are very good to me."

Pierrot sighed sadly and went away.

That evening, when Pantaloon was shut up in his study poring over medical books, Pierrot slipped out of the house and ran to Burattino's inn.

Pierrot was afraid that his errand might be a vain one. He thought that, after the events of the morning, Harlequin might have left town.

But Harlequin had no intention of doing so. No matter what happened, he was determined to remain near Columbine.

Pierrot poked his head through the open door of the inn where Scaramouch was playing for the guests and Violetta was serving them. He gazed quickly around the room and saw Harlequin sitting in a corner.

For the first time in his life, the dancer did not feel like playing tricks or dancing. He was saddened by many thoughts about Columbine. Would he ever meet her again? Would she marry him? If so, how could he get her away from the furious Pantaloon?

While he was thinking these thoughts, Harlequin saw Pierrot beckoning, and he went to him at once.

They went out into the dark street, and Pierrot told Harlequin how cruel Pantaloon was to Columbine, keeping her in her room and allowing her only dry bread to eat and water to to drink. "You must come to the house again, Harlequin."

"I mean to," said Harlequin firmly. "If only I could think of a way. But I am surprised to hear you talk like this, Pierrot. I should have thought you would have been glad to be rid of me."

Pierrot shook his head.

"I want Columbine to be happy," he said.

Harlequin seized him by the hand.

"What a good fellow you are," he said warmly. "I never expected to find a friend in you."

"I thought badly of you at first," said Pierrot, with a sad little smile. "But now I know it is only you who will make Columbine happy, so I have no choice but to help you if I can. And I think that perhaps I can. At least, I have a suggestion to make."

"What is it?" cried Harlequin eagerly.

"Well," said Pierrot, "of course it is out of the question for you to come to the house, or even within sight of it, in your own person. Pantaloon is not so shortsighted but that he would be sure to discover you—those clothes of yours make you so conspicuous—and I saw him loading his firearm this afternoon. He is not a bad marksman, either."

"What should I do, then?" Harlequin asked.

"You must disguise yourself," said Pierrot.

"Is that all you have to suggest?" said Harlequin, in tones of disappointment. "What would be the use, if no one is ever allowed inside Pantaloon's house?"

"I never thought of that," said Pierrot dejectedly, for he had considered his plan a good one. Though well-meaning, Pierrot was not very quick-witted.

"But is it really true that Pantaloon never lets anyone into his house?" asked Harlequin.

"Only his patients," replied Pierrot.

"Thank you," said Harlequin. "But I have had enough of Pantaloon's doctoring."

"Of course, there is Lelio, the rich nobleman whom Pantaloon hopes will marry Columbine," Pierrot went on. "Naturally he comes and goes as he chooses."

"Why, that is it!" exclaimed Harlequin. "I will disguise myself as Lelio."

"Oh, no!" cried Pierrot. "That would never do. What would happen if the real Lelio came while you were there?"

"Ahimè, that would cause a problem," Harlequin admitted. "But are you sure that Pantaloon has no other visitors than Lelio? Do none of Lelio's friends ever come, for instance?"

"No," said Pierrot, "none. Of course, Lelio has many servants as befits his noble rank, and sometimes he sends one with gifts for Columbine."

"Does he?" cried Harlequin joyfully. "Then I will disguise myself as Lelio's servant. Without my mask and with a great cloak over my shoulders, I could pass as one of his servants with a message from Lelio, couldn't I, Pierrot?" he hopefully asked.

"I suppose you could, Harlequin."

Harlequin slapped Pierrot on the back heartily. "You have earned my friendship forever," he cried. "If anyone should ever treat you badly, let me know and, by my mask, he shall feel this stick of mine!" he said, shaking it menacingly.

"Thank you very much, Harlequin," said Pierrot very softly.

And so it was that the very next morning Harlequin made his way once more to Pantaloon's house, this time disguised as Lelio's servant. He had removed his mask. Since no one had seen him without it, this, with a great black cloak covering his multicolored tight suit, completed his disguise.

Harlequin presented himself at Pantaloon's door. When the doctor himself cautiously opened it, Harlequin handed him a note which he had in his cloak pocket.

"Buon giorno, *Signor* Doctor," he said, "I am one of Signor Lelio's servants. I have here a note sent to you by my master."

Pantaloon suspiciously peered over his glasses at Harlequin and then glanced at the note. This is what he read:

My Dear Doctor;
I am very ill. Will you please come as soon as possible.
Lelio

After Pantaloon read the note, he again peered at Harlequin over the top of his thick glasses. "Should I believe the note or not?" was the thought that quickly flashed through his mind. However, he could not afford to take a chance of ignoring the message. What if Lelio, the richest nobleman in all Venice, were really ill? After all, he hoped that one day Lelio would marry his Columbine.

That settled it. "Tell your master that I will come as soon as I have gathered my bottles of medicines and as quickly as my legs will carry me." Then he shut the door in Harlequin's face.

Harlequin hid himself around the corner of a neighboring house, peeking out occasionally. Then, in a short while, he saw the doctor leave, shuffling on his way, clutching tightly his satchel of medicines. When he had disappeared, Harlequin moved quickly, and knocked at Pantaloon's door once more.

This time it was cautiously opened by Pierrot. "Well?" he asked.

"It is I, Harlequin. Oh, Pierrot, let me in. See, here is my mask," and he pulled out his black mask from his pocket. "It is I, Harlequin, without my mask on."

"Oh," cried Pierrot, for never having seen Harlequin without his mask, he did not know him. Then he said, "Quickly, come in."

When Pierrot had shut the door, he called to Columbine who hurried down the stairs.

Thus it was that Harlequin once again met the beautiful Columbine. He was very much grieved to see how unhappy she looked.

It was clear that at first she did not recognize him without his mask, but when he began to dance, then she knew him!

"Oh, my dear, dear Harlequin!" she exclaimed.

"My lovely Columbine. I only want to bring you happiness. Come with me and be my wife," said Harlequin. "We could be married right away. And just think, together we could travel from town to town and dance in the village squares for young and old through all of Italy. And at carnival time we would dress up and you, too, could wear a mask. Wouldn't that be fun, Columbine?"

"Yes, Harlequin, it would be fun!" said Columbine excitedly.

"Then hurry, come with me and together we shall dance, dance, dance, all our lives!" exclaimed Harlequin joyously.

Columbine ran from the room. When she returned, she was cloaked and carrying a little bag, in which she had put a few things which she wanted to take with her into her new life.

Pierrot saw them out. He tried to wish them a cheerful good-by, but as they disappeared into the morning, two big tears rolled down his white cheeks.

And so it was that Harlequin and Columbine were married in a little church just outside of Venice. They were happy together dancing to the tune of Scaramouch's lute. On and on the three of them traveled as a troupe, dancing and making music in the market places and at fairs in the piazzas: Harlequin, with his black mask and in his suit of multicolored, diamond-shaped patches and glittering spangles; Columbine, always lovely in her white dress and dancing shoes; and Scaramouch, who at long last had magnificent dancers to dance to his beautiful music.

Thus they journeyed on through Venice and throughout Italy and even France and England, on and on, always happy and gay.

About the Author

After receiving her Master of Library Science degree from Pratt Institute Library School, Rose Laura Mincieli was a children's librarian at the New York Public Library for twelve years, and the Queensborough Public Library for five years. At present she is a teacher-librarian in the Washington Street School in Franklin Square, New York where, in addition to storytelling, she adapts fairy tales and folk tales to puppetry and gives puppet shows.

In private life the author is Mrs. Frank Ross, Jr. She has previously published three books: a collection of original Italian folk tales, TALES MERRY AND WISE, PULCINELLA, OR PUNCH'S MERRY PRANKS and a retelling of selected tales from *Il Pentamerone* entitled OLD NEAPOLITAN FAIRY TALES.

The text of this book has been set on the Monotype in a type face named Bembo. The roman is a copy of a letter cut for the celebrated Venetian printer Aldus Manutius by Francesco Griffo, and first used in Cardinal Bembo's *De Aetna* of 1495—hence the name of the revival. Griffo's type is now generally recognized, thanks to the researches of Mr. Stanley Morison, to be the first of the old face group of types. The companion italic is an adaptation of a chancery script type designed by the Roman calligrapher and printer Lodovico degli Arrighi, called Vincentino, and used by him during the 1520's.

Composed by Westcott & Thomson, Inc., Philadelphia, Pa.
Printed by Halliday Lithograph Corp., West Hanover, Mass.
Bound by A. Horowitz & Son, Bookbinders, Clifton, N.J.
Typography by Atha Tehon